stop the clock
the anti-aging cookbook

Robyn Martin

RANDOM HOUSE
NEW ZEALAND

I dedicate this book to my dad. If only he had known what I have learnt, he may have had a long and healthy life reaping the happiness of his family's love, sharing their achievements and milestones.

Life inspires us to grow into our future, to challenge our genetics and never accept that we do not have the power to make a change.

Samuel James Matthews 3 May 1923 – 14 May 1992

A special thanks to Professor John Birkbeck for his assistance in checking the claims made in this book.

WEIGHT AND MEASURES
All recipes in this book have been tested using New Zealand standard measuring cups and spoons. All cup and spoon measures are level and brown sugar measures are firmly packed. Standard No. 6 eggs are used.

Crockery supplied by Smith & Caughey Limited

National Library of New Zealand Cataloguing-in-Publication Data
Martin, Robyn (Robyn Margaret)
Stop the clock : the anti-aging cookbook / Robyn Martin.
Includes index.
ISBN 1-86941-661-9
1. Cookery (Natural foods) 2. Aging-Prevention. I. Title.
641.563-dc 22

A RANDOM HOUSE BOOK
published by
Random House New Zealand
18 Poland Road, Glenfield, Auckland, New Zealand
www.randomhouse.co.nz

First published 2004

© 2004 Robyn Martin

The moral rights of the author have been asserted

ISBN 1 86941 661 9

Photography: Alan Gillard
Recipes tested by Virginia Hewin and Rosemary Hurdley
Design: Richard Wheatley, Red Design Limited
Printed in China

contents

introduction 4

the brain drain 6

keep 'em moving 28

mirror, mirror 48

boom ditty boom 68

the real oil 90

freedom fighting 112

little jack horner 132

introduction

We have all had a taste of the good life, those of us that enjoyed growing up in the forties, fifties and sixties. We shocked our families with the freedoms of the sixties, seventies and eighties and had our halcyon days forging a path in life and careers. We renovated the odd bungalow or villa along the way, had the babies, watched governments come and go, and now we have been put on a treadmill to miraculously stash away something for the third age – whatever that may be.

Amid all this, we still have a huge amount we want to do and we want to be able to do it in full working order. We all want to defy the aging process and get the most out of life. We want everything operating at its peak. The blunt and wonderful truth is we do not want to grow old. We want to have lots more birthdays and a fantastic quality of life that enables us to enjoy the new experiences and wisdom that come with age.

More and more we hear that we are what we eat. If you have had a poor diet you are probably feeling the effects of it now. The simple truth is that it is never too late to try to arrest the ravages of time and in some cases it is even possible to make amends.

The aging antidotes included in each chapter of this book are intended to highlight the importance of eating a wide variety of foods and emphasises foods of plant origin for their positive health benefits. No single food is the elixir of a long and healthy life. Instead, think of foods working together in a big chemical reaction to give your body the maximum possible health and anti-aging benefits. Making sure that chemical reaction is as beneficial as it possibly can be comes down to choosing the right foods.

This book is about eating the foods that will do just that – foods that will help slow the tick-tock of the clock. Many recipes have ingredients with a multitude of anti-aging benefits and the lists of foods at the beginning of each chapter will help you identify them.

This is a book that is all about making our food choices count, to defy the aging process with knowledge and enthusiasm, making sure we do get the most out of life.

To life!

important ingredients
to improve brain function

tuna	tomatoes	miso
salmon	cabbage	nuts
sardines	spinach	flaxseed oil
anchovies	broccoli	turmeric
kahawai	potatoes	ginkgo
chicken	soya beans	coffee
strawberries	soy milk	red wine
blueberries	tofu	beer
beetroot	tempeh	

the brain drain

I am probably speaking for many people of our generation, so aptly named the baby boomers, when I say that the thought of losing my marbles to Alzheimer's or another dementia sends chills down my spine.

Many of us have seen the demise of fine minds to these diseases. Some will even have nursed a loved one through the perils of a failing mind. None of us wants to go there – it is one tee-shirt we do not need.

The good news is that there are many everyday foods that have been proven to slow the degeneration of the brain caused by aging. If you know what they are it is easy to incorporate them into the list of foods you choose to eat regularly.

There is much research being done in this area and when new claims are made, take them on board. This is one part of the body for which surgical repair is not an option.

Straw-Blue Fruit Smoothie

Now don't turn your nose up at this. Smoothies are not just for youth! Try this for breakfast or, if you can't cope with that, perhaps have it as a snack with a sandwich at lunch or, at worst, use it as a cocktail base for that pre-dinner drink.

> 8–10 fresh or frozen strawberries
> 1 banana
> ½ cup fresh or frozen blueberries
> 1 tablespoon flaxseed oil
> 6 whole blanched almonds
> 2 tablespoons oat bran
> ½ cup trim milk or low-fat soy milk or fresh orange juice

Hull strawberries. Peel banana. Place strawberries, banana, blueberries, flaxseed oil, almonds and oat bran in a blender and blend until smooth. Add milk and blend. Serve chilled.

Serves 1

- Blueberries have been found to reverse some aspects of brain aging in animal studies. From a human perspective they are a no-risk way of having a crack at achieving the same result – try eating half a cup a day and see the benefits.

- When we use our brain we use energy, and one-third more oxygen than other body functions. This produces free radicals. We need antioxidants to scoop up these free radicals to prevent them damaging our brain. Berry fruit all have high levels of antioxidants. Blueberries, blackberries, cranberries, strawberries and raspberries provide wonderful protection for the brain.

Beetroot contains a host of beneficial vitamins, minerals and other compounds that help to energise the body and improve memory and concentration. These include beta-carotene (this is converted to vitamin A in the body), folic acid, vitamins B6 and C, manganese, calcium, magnesium, iron, potassium and phosphorus. Beetroot leaves are the best source of these nutrients.

Beetroot contains powerful antioxidants that help scoop up the free radicals, which have an adverse effect on brain aging. It is also thought to improve memory and concentration.

Beetroot, Spinach and Broccoli Salad

1 head broccoli
2 medium beetroot
2 large handfuls baby spinach
½ cup shelled pistachio nuts
3 tablespoons avocado oil
1 tablespoon red wine vinegar
freshly ground black pepper

Wash broccoli and cut into florets. Pour boiling water over broccoli and leave for 5 minutes. Drain and refresh under cold water and drain again. Peel beetroot and grate coarsely. Arrange washed spinach leaves over the base of a bowl or serving platter. Top with grated beetroot. Scatter over broccoli and pistachio nuts. Drizzle over avocado oil and vinegar. Grind over black pepper and serve.

Serves 6

Chicken and Vegetable Soup

1 onion
2 cloves garlic
1 tablespoon avocado oil
4 cups chicken stock
1 medium kumara
1 bunch spinach
1 head broccoli
1 carrot
200g boneless, skinless chicken
2 tomatoes

Peel onion and chop finely. Crush garlic, peel and chop finely. Heat avocado oil in a large saucepan and sauté onion and garlic for 5 minutes until clear but not coloured. Add chicken stock and bring to the boil. Peel kumara. Cut into chunks and add to stock mixture. Cover and cook for 10 minutes or until kumara is cooked. Wash and trim spinach. Wash broccoli and cut into small florets. Scrub carrot and cut into slices. Cut chicken into bite-sized pieces. Cut tomatoes into small cubes. When kumara is cooked, mash coarsely in the liquid with a potato masher. Bring to the boil and add spinach, broccoli, carrot and chicken. Cook for 5 minutes or until chicken is cooked. Serve topped with tomatoes.

Serves 4

- Carrots have a high level of beta-carotene, which converts to vitamin A in the body. They are being investigated for their help in retaining memory, because the area of the brain that specialises in memory function cannot operate without vitamin A.

- Broccoli is an excellent source of lipoic acid, which is claimed to increase energy and brain power. Tomatoes are also a good source of lipoic acid.

Curcumin, the pigment that makes turmeric yellow, has a powerful anti-inflammatory effect. Inflammation is being investigated as a possible contributor to Alzheimer's disease. Turmeric has also been shown to reduce plaques in the brain that cause Alzheimer's disease.

The long-chain omega-3 fatty acids found in fish oils are essential for normal brain function.

Fish Cakes with Indian Tomato Sauce

185g can tuna in water
1 red onion
1 tablespoon oil
120g packet baby spinach
2 teaspoons turmeric
1 tablespoon ground linseeds
2 cups cold mashed potato
2 tablespoons Thai flavour base
3 tablespoons olive oil
400g can Indian-style tomatoes

Drain tuna. Peel onion and chop finely. Heat oil in a frying pan and sauté onion over a medium heat for 5 minutes or until soft. Add washed spinach and turmeric and stir until spinach wilts. Mix tuna, onion mixture, linseeds, potato and Thai flavour base together until well combined. Shape half cups of mixture into patties. Heat oil in a frying pan. Cook patties over a medium heat until lightly golden. Turn and cook second side. While patties are cooking, heat tomatoes. Serve patties with Indian tomatoes.

Serves 2 to 3

Anti trach.

Smoked Salmon, Spinach and Egg Pies

2 sheets ready-rolled soy and linseed pastry
1 bunch spinach
200g wood-roasted smoked salmon
2 tablespoons capers
2 tablespoons chopped fresh dill
4 eggs

Cut each pastry sheet in half on the diagonal. Place on an oven tray. Wash spinach and trim. Pour boiling water over. Drain spinach, removing as much water as possible. Remove bones from salmon with clean tweezers and remove skin. Mix salmon, capers, dill and spinach together in a bowl. Divide mixture among the four pastry pieces, placing at the right-angled corner of the pastry triangle. Wet edges of pastry and fold points of long side over the filling to the right-angled point and seal. Open the slit in the middle of the pies and break an egg into each. Break the egg yolk with a knife. Bake at 200°C for 25 to 30 minutes, or until pastry is golden and cooked.

Serves 4

- Spinach is one of the better food sources of glutathione and alpha-lipoic acid, which are important antioxidants in the body. Glutathione is found in the watery cell interior. It protects the DNA in our cells from oxidation. Alpha-lipoic acid helps cells absorb an amino acid essential for the body to make glutathione. It helps strengthen the memory and turns off genes that can accelerate aging.

- Oily fish feature heavily in all aspects of anti-aging health. Knowing the oil content of your favourite fish is important if your fish-eating objective is to have the advantage of omega-3 fatty acids in your diet.

Fish oils are essential for normal brain function. Low fish consumption has been linked to a range of psychiatric disorders.

Nuts are a good source of vitamin E, which acts as an antioxidant and helps prevent Alzheimer's disease.

Crusty Salmon with Grilled Tomatoes and Oregano

2 serving-sized pieces salmon fillet
¼ cup chopped mixed nuts
2 tablespoons sun-dried tomato pesto
3 medium tomatoes
freshly ground black pepper
fresh oregano leaves
baby spinach leaves

Remove bones from salmon with clean tweezers and remove skin if preferred. Place fish on a piece of baking paper on an oven tray. Mix nuts and pesto together. Spread over top surface of salmon. Cut tomatoes in half around the equator (not through stem end). Grind black pepper over cut surfaces and place on oven tray. Grill salmon and tomatoes for 5 minutes under a hot grill or on fan grill at 200°C until salmon is still slightly rare and tomatoes heated through. Sprinkle tomatoes with oregano and serve with baby spinach leaves.

Serves 2

Fresh Tuna Loin with Wasabi and Anchovy Mayo

400g piece fresh tuna loin
1 tablespoon avocado oil
1 teaspoon garlic salt
1 bunch spinach

Brush the tuna with avocado oil and sprinkle lightly with garlic salt. Grill or barbecue each side for 1 to 2 minutes depending on the thickness of the fish. (The inside of the tuna should be rare.) Cover and stand for 5 minutes. Wash spinach and cook in a saucepan with just the water clinging to the leaves for 2 to 3 minutes or until bright green and wilted. Drain, pressing out as much water as possible. Cut tuna into 0.5cm thick slices. Arrange on top of spinach and top with Wasabi and Anchovy Mayo.

Wasabi and Anchovy Mayo

50g tin anchovies in oil
½ cup low-fat mayonnaise
½ teaspoon wasabi powder
1 tablespoon chopped chives

Mash anchovies in 1 tablespoon of their oil. Mix in mayonnaise, wasabi and chives.

Serves 2

- Fish oils help improve memory and brain function.

- Fish that have high oil-content include anchovies, kahawai, mackerel, mullet, sardines, salmon, sprats and albacore tuna.

- Fish that have medium-to-high oil-content include kingfish, orange roughy, warehou, skipjack and southern bluefin tuna, and marlin.

- There are indications that blueberries may prevent or delay the onset of Alzheimer's disease.

- Large amounts of alcohol kill brain cells.

- Researchers have found that protein deposits form on the brains of people with Alzheimer's disease. Foods rich in vitamin E such as wheat germ, nuts and oils are being studied for their role in preventing the formation of these protein deposits on the brain — another good reason to include vitamin E-rich foods in your diet.

Very Berry Sorbet

As you get older, one of the hardest things is to maintain your weight, do your bit for God and the Queen and enjoy all the delicious foods we have on offer. Ice-cream doesn't fit into a regular regime but a sorbet that packs a punch can make an enjoyable, delicious substitute. Try this for size.

> 500g mixture of fresh or free-flow frozen blueberries, strawberries, raspberries and blackberries
> ¼ cup lime cordial
> 1 cup fresh orange juice
> 1 egg white

Mash fresh or frozen berries in a bowl. Mix in lime cordial and orange juice. Pour into a shallow freezer-proof container. Freeze until almost solid. Turn into a food processor. Add egg white. Alternatively, break frozen berry mixture into pieces in a bowl and add egg white. Process or beat with an eggbeater until combined. Cover and refreeze until frozen. If you are going to store this in the freezer make sure the surface of the sorbet is covered with plastic wrap to prevent ice crystals forming.

Serves 6

Fresh Berry Terrine

    2½ cups cranberry juice
    3 tablespoons gelatine
    2 cups fresh or frozen raspberries
    2 cups fresh or frozen blueberries
    16 sponge fingers

Take ¼ cup from the measured cranberry juice. Sprinkle gelatine over and soak for 5 minutes. Dissolve in a bowl over hot water or in the microwave on high for 10 seconds. Stir into remaining cranberry juice. Mix in fresh or thawed berries. Line the base and sides of a straight-sided 6-cup-capacity dish with sponge fingers, rounded side out. Pour in fruit mixture. Cover and refrigerate until set. Trim ends of sponge fingers that are above jelly level. To serve, dip dish into hot water and turn onto a serving plate. Serve with yoghurt or your favourite low-fat ice cream.

Serves 8

- Buy fruits and vegetables with the best, brightest colour. If they are meant to be red, make sure you buy the brightest red – not half green. When fruits and vegetables are ripe they provide the optimum amount of antioxidants, minerals and vitamins. For example, blueberries can triple their level of natural antioxidants from the time they first turn blue to reaching full ripeness.

- Research has shown that blueberries slow, and in some cases reverse, damage in aging brains, improving short-term memory and coordination.

Fresh Blueberry Sauce

2 cups fresh blueberries
¼ cup blueberry jam
3 tablespoons water

Place blueberries, jam and water in a blender or food processor. Blend or process until berries are lightly crushed.

Makes 1 ¼ cups

Chocolate contains powerful antioxidants called catechins and the secret to tapping into these antioxidants is to buy good quality dark chocolate. The more cocoa solids in the chocolate, the greater the antioxidants present. Anything less that 35 per cent chocolate and you are kidding yourself about the 'treat with a health benefit'.

Despite all the negatives said about coffee, having two to three cups a day reduces the risk of Alzheimer's disease.

Mocha Dessert Cake with Fresh Blueberry Sauce

Looking after your health doesn't mean you have to eat mung beans and chant. Nor do you have to become a health-food guru. The important ingredients for brain health can be incorporated in your diet with ease once you know what they are.

1 cup boiling water
¼ cup ground coffee
150g butter
100g cooking chocolate
¾ cup sugar
3 eggs
2 teaspoons vanilla essence
2 cups flour
2 teaspoons baking powder
1 teaspoon baking soda
¼ cup cocoa

Line the base of a deep, 20cm round cake tin with baking paper. Pour water over coffee grounds in a plunger or jug. Leave for 5 minutes to steep. Plunge or strain coffee liquid. Melt butter in a saucepan large enough to mix all the ingredients. Remove from heat. Mix in chocolate and coffee and stir to melt chocolate. Add sugar, eggs and vanilla. Beat well with a wooden spoon until combined. Sift in flour, baking powder, baking soda and cocoa. Mix to combine. Pour the mixture into cake tin. Bake at 180°C for 45 minutes, or until cake springs back when lightly touched. Leave in tin for 10 minutes before turning onto a cooling rack. Serve with Fresh Blueberry Sauce and cream (optional).

Serves 10

important ingredients for joints and mobility

all vegetables
watercress
spinach
beetroot
egg whites
tuna
salmon
sardines
anchovies
kahawai
shellfish
avocado
bananas

sour cherries
cherry juice
lemons
nuts
beans
lentils
wholegrain bread
wholegrain cereals
oats
sesame seeds
sunflower seeds
pumpkin seeds
cider vinegar

flaxseed oil
honey
fresh ginger
turmeric
rosemary
soya beans
soy milk
tofu
tempeh
miso
brown rice
white rice
wild rice

keep 'em moving

There is an image in my head that would provide a new business opportunity for an aging entrepreneur; it is that rest homes have been replaced by rest resorts — places to go to rest from busy, active lives. So I am starting a movement here to arm people with the knowledge they need to eat their way to joint-health so that they experience a minimum of aches and pains and can be active as they age.

    Do not tell me this is unrealistic — you are talking to someone who was told in her youth that she would be in a wheelchair by the age of 25. I am already a couple of decades past that and do a 6km walk three times a week, yoga, regular Pilates classes and I love aqua aerobics. Is there anything else to say?

Almond and Oatmeal Hotcakes with Honeyed Bananas

For a change try serving these delicious hotcakes with other seasonal fruit such as strawberries, blueberries and fresh crisp apples.

½ cup flour
1 cup oatmeal
2 teaspoons baking powder
¼ cup ground almonds
1 egg
1 cup low-fat soy milk
oil
4 small bananas
¼ cup runny honey
natural low-fat yoghurt

Mix flour, oatmeal, baking powder and almonds together in a bowl. Lightly beat egg and soy milk together. Pour into dry ingredients and mix to combine. Cook half cups of mixture in a hot, oiled pan. When golden and bubbles appear on top surface, turn and cook second side. Keep warm. Peel bananas and heat in an oiled pan or place in a dish in the microwave on high power for one minute. Serve hotcakes with banana, runny honey and yoghurt.

Serves 4

- The protein, calcium and phosphorus in oats all help build strong bones and connective tissue.

- The healing properties of honey help speed up recovery from joint damage and arthritis.

- Don't peel your apples. Apple skins contain important flavonoids that fight inflammation.

- Blueberries contain potent anti-inflammatory chemicals that help relieve arthritic pain.

- Strawberries help soothe arthritic pain caused by inflammation.

Anecdotal reports tell of people suffering from arthritis-related pain gaining major relief from eating sour cherries or drinking sour cherry juice. Researchers are looking at the anti-inflammatory effect of anthocyanin pigments in cherries to see if they block the action of the enzymes that cause arthritic pain.

Bananas are one of the best sources of potassium, which helps slow the loss of calcium from the bones.

Tarzan's Joint Juice

This is a great way to start the day and, yes, it will help you swing from the trees! Make your own combination of juice in the blender or a juicer, choosing from any of these fresh fruits: cherries, banana, orange, pawpaw, pineapple, kiwifruit, guava. Carrot can be used too but is best done in a juicer. Add fresh ginger if wished for an even better brew.

> 1 cup cranberry juice
> 1 kiwifruit
> 1 large wedge pawpaw
> 1 banana

Place cranberry juice in a blender. Peel kiwifruit, pawpaw and banana. Chop roughly and add to blender. Blend until smooth, adding ice cubes for a well-chilled drink. Serve immediately.

Serves 1

Asian Seafood and Rice Noodle Soup

1 onion
2 cloves garlic
1 tablespoon avocado oil
1 tablespoon grated fresh ginger
1 tablespoon Thai green curry paste
6 cups fish stock
2 kaffir lime leaves
2 skinned and boned fish fillets
2 heads spinach
1 cup shelled prawns
2 tablespoons chopped fresh coriander
125g rice stick noodles
snow pea sprouts

Peel onion, halve and cut into thin slices. Crush, peel and chop garlic. Heat oil in a saucepan or clay pot. Sauté onion, garlic and ginger for 5 minutes or until soft. Add curry paste and cook for about one minute until fragrant. Add stock and bring to the boil. Cut central rib from lime leaves and slice leaves finely. Add to stock. Cut fish into chunks. Wash spinach and chop roughly. Add fish, spinach, prawns and coriander to stock and simmer for 2 to 3 minutes or until fish is just cooked. Cook noodles to packet instructions. Drain and divide among four bowls. Pour fish mixture over noodles. Garnish with snow pea sprouts. Add a whole, cooked, shell-on prawn if wished.

Serves 4

- Fish oils help reduce joint swelling, reducing pain for sufferers of rheumatoid arthritis.

- Fresh tuna is a good food to eat to prevent and alleviate rheumatoid arthritis. It contains beneficial omega-3 fatty acids, biotin and niacin, which have an anti-inflammatory effect in the body.

- Ginger has a strong anti-inflammatory effect, helping relieve arthritic pain.

Cabbage is rich in minerals, including calcium for strong bones, function of the nervous system and muscles, and magnesium, which also promotes healthy muscles.

Spinach contains calcium, magnesium and manganese — elements that help people with osteoarthritis.

Foods rich in potassium and magnesium contribute to greater bone density. Potassium is found in bananas, oranges, broccoli and pawpaw. Magnesium is found in dark breads, orange juice, fish, spinach, chicken and nuts.

Green Goddess and Garlic Soup

    1 bunch watercress or 1 large bunch spinach
    1 leek
    4 cabbage leaves
    ½ iceberg lettuce
    6 cloves garlic
    6 cups chicken stock
    6 sprigs parsley
    1 bay leaf
    1 sprig thyme
    ½ cup brown rice
    wholegrain bread

Wash watercress or spinach and trim stalks if necessary. Trim leek and cut into wide slices. Cut thick core from cabbage and discard. Roughly chop cabbage and lettuce. Crush and peel garlic. Bring chicken stock to the boil in a large saucepan. Add vegetables, garlic, parsley, bay leaf, thyme and brown rice. Cover and cook for 20 minutes, or until rice is cooked. Blend or process until smooth. Serve with croutons of toasted wholegrain bread.

Serves 4

Delicious Look-defying Lentil Salad

Now don't turn the page and say lentils aren't for you. This salad is absolutely delicious even if brown lentils don't make the top ten most appetising-looking foods. If you have a couple of sweet potatoes on hand try adding them, cooked and cubed, to this salad.

> 1 cup brown lentils
> 1 cup precooked whole wheat
> 3 spring onions
> 1 clove garlic
> 1 tablespoon grated fresh ginger
> 1 tablespoon curry powder
> 2 tablespoons chopped fresh mint
> ¼ cup chopped parsley
> ¼ cup cider vinegar
> ⅛ cabbage
> ½ teaspoon salt

Wash lentils and place in a saucepan with cold water to cover. Bring to the boil and cook for 35 to 40 minutes or until tender. Drain and place in a bowl. Cook the precooked wheat to packet instructions. Drain and add to lentils. Trim spring onions and cut into 1cm slices. Crush, peel and chop garlic finely. Mix spring onions, garlic, ginger, curry powder, mint, parsley and vinegar into lentil mixture. Toss to coat. Wash cabbage and shred finely. Toss through salad with salt just before serving.

Serves 6

- Curcumin, the pigment that makes the turmeric used in curry powder yellow, is both a strong antioxidant and anti-inflammatory. It blocks the release of inflammatory enzymes in the cells — an action that some well-known arthritis drugs try to mimic.

- The protein, calcium, magnesium, potassium and phosphorus in sweet potatoes help maintain healthy bones, muscles and nerves.

- Mixing parsley, ginger, cayenne or fennel with dishes made from dried beans and lentils may help alleviate flatulence, which some people suffer as a side effect from eating these foods.

- The best sources of essential fatty acids and omega-3 fatty acids are wheatgerm oil, canola oil, evening primrose oil, cod liver oil, flaxseed oil and other fish oils.

- Fat is essential in the diet as it carries the fat-soluble vitamins A, D, E and K.

Salmon Puffs with Chopped Egg and Avocado

Serve these as finger food or change the bread to wholegrain toast and serve as a light meal for lunch or tea.

> 2 slices dark rye bread
> 210g can salmon
> 1 egg white
> 1 avocado
> 1 hard-boiled egg
> 2 tablespoons chopped parsley

Toast one side of rye bread. Drain salmon and remove bones. Beat egg white until stiff. Fold salmon into egg white and pile on top of untoasted side of rye bread. Grill until puffed and browned. Peel and destone avocado. Slice flesh into thin strips. Shell boiled egg and chop finely. Arrange avocado slices and chopped egg on bread slices. Garnish with chopped parsley.

Makes 2

Fresh Pineapple Salsa for Chicken or Fish

    1 avocado
    ½ fresh pineapple
    ¼ pawpaw
    1 tablespoon grated fresh ginger
    1 tablespoon chopped fresh coriander
    1 tablespoon chopped fresh mint
    ¼ teaspoon prepared minced chilli

Peel and destone avocado. Chop flesh into cubes. Peel and core pineapple. Cut flesh into small cubes. Peel and deseed pawpaw. Cut flesh into small cubes. Mix avocado, pineapple, pawpaw, ginger, coriander, mint and chilli together. Serve with steamed or grilled chicken or fish.

Makes approximately 2 cups

- Chillies contain a chemical called capsaicin, which has a pain-relieving effect. It is helpful for general aches and pains.

- Avocados contain glutathione, which helps prevent rheumatoid arthritis.

If you suffer from gout, avoid all animal foods and, some say, mushrooms, asparagus, spinach, artichokes, beans and peas. Alcohol is also off limits.

If you are overweight you increase your risk of developing osteoarthritis, particularly in weight-bearing joints. Maintaining a healthy weight will improve mobility as you age.

Banana and Cracked Wheat Muffins

¼ cup cracked wheat
1 cup boiling water
1 cup wholemeal flour
½ cup flour
4 teaspoons baking powder
2 teaspoons ground ginger
2 ripe bananas
¼ cup honey
1 tablespoon avocado oil
1¼ cups non-fat milk or 1 cup low-fat soy milk and ¼ cup water

Place cracked wheat in a bowl. Pour over boiling water and set aside for 5 minutes. Drain. Mix wholemeal flour, flour, baking powder and ginger together in a bowl. Mash bananas with honey and avocado oil. Add milk or soy milk and water. Mix to combine. Make a well in the centre of the dry ingredients. Add banana mixture and cracked wheat. Mix quickly to just combine. Three-quarters fill greased muffin tins with mixture. Bake at 200°C for 20 to 25 minutes or until muffins spring back when lightly touched. Remove from oven and cover with a tea towel. Stand for 5 minutes before turning onto a cooling rack.

Makes 10

Italian Honey Nut Panforte

1 cup honey
1 tablespoon grated orange rind
2 teaspoons grated lemon rind
1 cup chopped toasted almonds
¼ cup toasted sesame seeds
2 cups soft wholemeal omega-3 DHA-enriched breadcrumbs
1 teaspoon fresh rosemary leaves
½ teaspoon orange flower water

Oil a 20cm round cake tin and dust with icing sugar. Heat honey and orange and lemon rinds for 5 minutes in a saucepan large enough to mix all the ingredients. Add almonds, sesame seeds, breadcrumbs, rosemary and orange flower water. Stir continuously over a medium heat for 3 minutes or until the mixture stiffens and comes away from the sides of the saucepan. Turn into cake tin. Press the top with wet hands to smooth, but take care as the mixture will be hot. Leave until cold. Turn out and cut small wedges to serve. Store in the fridge or freezer.

- Nuts have anti-inflammatory properties, which help reduce the symptoms of rheumatoid arthritis.

- Sesame seeds contain high levels of vitamin E, which is essential for muscle health. A lack of vitamin E leads to muscle wastage.

important ingredients to maintain good skin

citrus fruit
strawberries
berries
pawpaw
mango
apples
kiwifruit
pears
avocado
broccoli
cabbage
watercress
spinach
pumpkin
capsicums
carrots
beetroot

yams
sweet potatoes (kumara)
mushrooms
tuna
salmon
sardines
anchovies
kahawai
oysters
mussels
seaweed products
olive oil
sesame seeds
sunflower seeds
pumpkin seeds
lentils
Brazil nuts

hazelnuts
almonds
walnuts
oats
chickpeas
wheat germ
wholemeal bread
soya beans
soy milk
tofu
tempeh
miso
liver
garlic
dark beer
brewer's yeast

mirror, mirror

The visible signs of aging are probably the saddest evidence that there is a tick in that old clock. I have always thought that the sight loss that often comes with aging is actually a kind way of preserving self-esteem. It was confirmed when I made the mistake of putting on my glasses in the full glare of an over-lit mirror. Woe is me! Is this what the rest of the world sees?

Maintaining fantastic skin is a challenge, especially for those of us who did the sixties and seventies version of a sun-dried tomato, baking in the sun with lashings of baby oil in pursuit of that film-star tan. Sure, some got it, but the rest of us just hoped for a freckle merger. Minimising the long-term effects of sunburn and eating foods that enhance skin health are important to how we all feel, especially as we approach and celebrate birthdays.

You may not be able to turn back the clock but you may be able to slow it by knowing what foods you can enjoy to defy the lines of time.

A Skinful for Breakfast

For a change, add blueberries when they are in season.

>   1 orange
>   6 strawberries
>   ½ mango
>   1 slice pawpaw

Peel orange using a small knife, taking as much pith from the flesh as possible. Cut orange into segments between membranes. Do this over a bowl to retain juice. Hull strawberries. Cut in half if large. Add to orange slices. Peel mango and cut into slices. Peel and deseed pawpaw. Cut flesh into cubes. Mix the fruit together. Place in serving bowls. Sprinkle over Oaty Topping and serve with extra juice, soy milk or yoghurt if preferred.

Oaty Topping

>   2 tablespoons Brazil nuts
>   2 tablespoons almonds
>   ½ cup rolled oats
>   1 tablespoon wheat germ

Finely chop Brazil nuts and almonds. Mix nuts, oats and wheat germ together.

Serves 3

- Berries contain all the essential antioxidants — vitamins A, C and E — that help prevent premature aging. These vitamins have a cleansing function, which is great for the skin.

- Blueberries are rich in anthocyanins, which give the blueberries their blue colour and help to keep your skin looking young and healthy.

- We all know oranges are a good source of vitamin C. What is less widely known is that vitamin C is important in making collagen, which keeps the skin in good shape, defying the sagging that can come with aging.

- Soy products help build and maintain collagen and elastin in the skin, making it firm, full and youthful.

The antioxidants in spinach help reduce the risk of skin cancers.

Most nuts help maintain good skin and prevent wrinkles because they are a good source of essential fatty acids.

Roasted Mushrooms with Nutty Topping

4 large brown flat mushrooms
2 cloves garlic
1 tablespoon tahini
1 tablespoon wheat germ
¼ cup chopped walnuts
1 bunch spinach
2 slices wholegrain bread
120g blue cheese or feta
fresh pear slices to garnish

Wipe mushrooms and remove stalks. Trim stalks and chop finely. Crush, peel and chop garlic. Mix mushroom stalks, tahini, garlic, wheat germ and walnuts together. Place on gill side of mushrooms. Bake, covered, at 200°C for 10 minutes. Remove cover and grill tops until golden. Wash spinach and cook in a saucepan for 3 to 5 minutes with just the water clinging to the leaves. Squeeze out as much water as possible. Toast bread and place one slice on each plate. Top with spinach and mushrooms. Crumble cheese over and garnish with fresh pear slices.

Serves 2

Avocado Skin-tonic Salad with Roasted Capsicum Vinaigrette

2 avocados
1 roasted red capsicum
1 apple
1 pear
½ cup roasted hazelnuts
watercress or baby spinach

Peel and destone avocado. Cut flesh into slices. Cut red pepper into strips. Cut apple and pear into quarters. Remove cores and slice. Mix avocado, capsicum, apple, pear and hazelnuts together. Gently toss through vinaigrette. Serve on top of watercress or spinach leaves.

Roasted Capsicum Vinaigrette

1 roasted red capsicum
2 tablespoons lemon juice
2 tablespoons avocado oil

Place capsicum, lemon juice and avocado oil in a blender or food processor and process until combined. Alternatively, sieve capsicum to a purée and mix with juice and oil.

Serves 6

- Avocados contain vitamin E, which strengthens collagen in the skin.

- The antioxidant vitamins A, C and E and zinc are all found in capsicums and there are higher levels in red capsicums. Red capsicums are, as a result, particularly good for the skin.

Fish oils help improve dry skin and inflammatory skin conditions like dermatitis and eczema. Some claims have even been made that they reduce cellulite.

The essential fatty acids found in fish prevent dry skin, hair and nails. They also enhance the normal function of the reproductive system.

Salmon and Noodle Salad

>125g soba noodles
>200g cooked salmon fillet or smoked salmon
>2 spring onions
>½ telegraph cucumber or 1 Lebanese cucumber
>1 red onion
>½ cup fresh coriander leaves
>1 cup fresh mint leaves
>1 handful baby spinach leaves
>1 handful rocket
>1 handful watercress

Cook noodles to packet instructions. Cool. Remove bones from salmon with clean tweezers and remove skin. Cut into chunks. Trim spring onions and slice finely. Cut cucumber in half lengthwise. Remove seeds and cut flesh into chunks. Peel onion and slice finely. Mix spring onions, cucumber, onion, coriander, mint, spinach, rocket and watercress together. Toss well. Arrange salad mixture on serving plates. Top with noodles and salmon. Drizzle dressing over and serve.

Dressing

>½ teaspoon prepared minced chilli
>¼ cup avocado oil
>½ teaspoon wasabi powder
>1 tablespoon grated fresh ginger
>½ cup lime juice

Mix chilli, oil, wasabi, ginger and lime juice together until combined.

Serves 4

Indian Chicken and Mango Stir-fry

1 onion
2 cloves garlic
2 spring onions
1 carrot
¼ Chinese or savoy cabbage
1 head broccoli
300g can chickpeas
1 fresh mango
1 tablespoon sesame oil
1 tablespoon curry powder
200g chicken tenderloins
1 cup chicken stock
1 tablespoon chopped fresh parsley or coriander
mango chutney
poppadoms

Peel onion and cut into rings. Crush, peel and chop garlic. Trim spring onions and cut into 2cm pieces on the diagonal. Scrub carrot, trim and cut into thin strips. Wash cabbage and shred finely. Wash broccoli and cut into florets. Drain chickpeas. Peel mango and cut into slices. Heat oil in a wok or frying pan. Stir-fry onion, garlic, spring onions, carrot and broccoli for 5 minutes. Add curry powder and cook for 1 minute or until spices smell fragrant. Add cabbage and chicken and stir-fry for 2 minutes or until chicken is almost cooked. Add chickpeas and chicken stock. Cook for 2 minutes or until chicken is cooked and stock hot. Serve garnished with coriander and accompanied by mango chutney and poppadoms.

Serves 4

- Mangos are rich in vitamins C and E — both vitamins that are good for the skin. It also contains the carotenoid beta-cryptoxanthin, which is thought to help protect against skin damage caused by the sun. Papaya is the best source of beta-cryptoxanthin.

- Mangos and pawpaws (papayas) are like internal vacuum cleaners, detoxifying the body, resulting in improved skin texture. As well as beta-carotene they contain vitamins C and E, which are also great for good skin.

Onions, garlic and eggplant contain polyphenols, which help protect the skin.

One mango contains about 160 percent of our daily requirement of beta-carotene, 95 percent of vitamin C and 10 percent of vitamin E — all essential vitamins for skin health.

Favourite Fish with Lime, Mint and Mango Salsa

Choose your favourite fish for this dish, remembering that oily fish are better for your skin. You can use pawpaw if mango is not available.

>   300g fillet of your favourite fish
>   2 fresh limes
>   1 clove garlic
>   1 tablespoon Thai fish sauce
>   ¼ cup chopped fresh mint
>   ½ teaspoon prepared minced chilli
>   1 kaffir lime leaf
>   1 mango
>   2 tablespoons chopped fresh coriander
>   noodles cooked to packet instructions

Prepare fish as necessary, removing skin and bones. Cut into portion-sized pieces. Squeeze juice from limes and place in a bowl. Crush, peel and finely chop garlic. Add to juice with fish sauce, mint and chilli. Remove central vein from lime leaf and chop leaf finely. Add to bowl. Peel mango and cut into small chunks. Add to bowl with coriander and mix to combine. Grill fish for 2 minutes, depending on thickness of fish, or until just cooked. Serve fish on cooked noodles, topped with mango salsa.

Serves 2

boom ditty boom

My family has a genetic predisposition to heart disease, and having seen the demise of my dear dad to this disease, I have been determined to defy any negative heart genes I may have inherited. Genetics only has a 25 percent impact on your prognosis for life and it is 25 percent you can make sure you try to control.

Knowledge and choice make having a healthy heart a real option for those who want to get the most from life. Eating foods that will help, maintaining a healthy weight and exercising regularly are all simple and enjoyable choices to make sure you give the most important organ of your body the treatment it deserves.

Awareness of the foods that promote heart-health is the first step to making choices that will keep your ticker going 'boom ditty boom'. Incorporating these into your meal choices is easy and, believe me, it is never too late to make changes that will have a positive impact on your heart-health.

The secret is choosing foods that count — foods that taste fantastic and have a health benefit, while you enjoy a delicious eating experience.

Toasted Breakfast Muffins with Fresh Fruit

1 apple
1 pear
1 orange
1 kiwifruit
2 passionfruit or ¼ cup unsweetened passionfruit pulp
2 cinnamon flavoured English muffins
low-fat yoghurt or soy yoghurt
2 tablespoons chopped hazelnuts

Wash fruit. Cut apple and pear into quarters. Remove cores and cut into thin slices. Place in a bowl. Peel orange using a small knife, taking as much pith from the flesh as possible. Cut orange into segments between membranes. Do this over the bowl the apple and pear are in to catch the juice. Peel kiwifruit and cut into chunks. Mix passionfruit pulp into fruit mixture. Slit muffins and toast. Place a muffin half on a serving plate. Top with fruit mixture. Serve with low-fat yoghurt. Sprinkle with hazelnuts.

Serves 4

- Bananas and oranges are potassium-rich foods which help regulate blood pressure.

- Soy products help lower high blood-pressure and cholesterol levels.

- Mangos and cantaloupe contain the heart-helping vitamin C and folate as well as potassium.

- Red pigments in cranberries are thought to reduce the risk of heart-attack-inducing blood clots.

- Green tea has much less caffeine than regular tea and also contains vitamins, minerals and some powerful antioxidants known as polyphenols. These antioxidants scoop up disease-causing free radicals and can help reduce blood pressure.

- Eat your almonds with the skins on as the polyphenols in almond skins help prevent atherosclerosis.

Winter Fruit Salad

Use this for breakfast or dessert. It is delicious anytime. Choose dried fruits that are free of preservatives.

1 cup dried dates
1 cup dried figs
1 cup stoned prunes
1 cup sticky raisins
1 cup dried apricots
skin of 1 orange
3 cups hot green tea
slivered almonds

Cut dates and figs in half if large. Place in a non-metallic bowl with prunes, raisins and apricots. Using a zester, remove thin strips of rind from the orange. Alternatively, thinly pare the rind from the orange, avoiding the pith, and cut the rind into thin strips. Add to fruit. Pour green tea over. Leave to soak. Cover and refrigerate until ready to serve. Serve sprinkled with slivered almonds.

Serves 8

Kumara and Watercress Vichyssoise

Use spinach if watercress is unavailable.

1 onion
2 cloves garlic
1 tablespoon avocado or olive oil
2 sticks celery
2 cups chicken stock
2 cups miso
2 kumara
1 bunch watercress

Peel onion and chop roughly. Crush, peel and chop garlic. Heat oil in a large saucepan and sauté onion and garlic for 5 minutes or until soft. Trim celery and chop. Add to pan and sauté for 2 minutes. Add stock and miso and bring to the boil. Peel kumara and cut into pieces. Add to stock mixture. Cover and cook for 10 minutes. Wash watercress. Pureé soup in a blender or food processor with watercress. Reheat if necessary before serving.

Serves 4

Garlic improves heart-health. It can help lower cholesterol levels and high blood-pressure, and reduce clotting. It also cleanses and tones the liver.

Kumara (sweet potatoes) are not just the carbohydrate fix we thought. The darker their orange colour, the more antioxidants they contain. The antioxidants they contain are vitamins A and C, and zinc. Antioxidants trap free radicals before they damage our cells.

※ The selenium and essential fatty acids in oily fish help protect against heart disease.

※ Spinach is a rich source of folate, which helps prevent heart disease by disposing of the amino acid homocysteine. Homocysteine is ranked by some scientists as being as significant as cholesterol and smoking in its contribution to heart disease.

Sardine Lunch Toasties

3 slices wholegrain bread
106g can sardines in tomato sauce
1 egg white
1 carrot
1 large handful baby spinach leaves
1 tablespoon lemon juice
freshly ground black pepper

Toast wholegrain bread on one side. Mash sardines. Beat egg white until soft peaks form. Fold sardine mixture into egg white. Divide mixture among bread slices, spreading on untoasted side of wholegrain bread. Grill until puffed and lightly golden. Scrub carrot and grate. Remove toast from oven. Place each slice on a serving plate. Top with baby spinach then grated carrot. Drizzle lemon juice over and grind black pepper over. Serve immediately.

Makes 3

Curried Kumara, Banana and Broccoli Salad

3 medium kumara
1 head broccoli
4 spring onions
2 bananas
½ cup lemon juice
1 tablespoon tahini
2 teaspoons curry powder
½ cup avocado or olive oil
2 tablespoons chopped chives

Peel kumara and cut into pieces. Boil or steam for 15 to 20 minutes or until tender. Drain and cool. Cut into cubes. Place in a large bowl. Wash broccoli and cut into florets. Blanch in boiling water for 3 minutes. Drain and refresh under cold water and drain again. Add to bowl. Cut spring onions into diagonal slices. Peel bananas and cut into diagonal slices. Toss in lemon juice. Add spring onions, and bananas to bowl. Mix tahini, curry powder and avocado or olive oil together. Gently mix through vegetable and banana mixture. Scatter chives over.

Serves 4

- The lutein in broccoli helps protect against atherosclerosis.

- The organosulfur compounds in onions and garlic are thought to be more potent than aspirin in thinning the blood, thereby helping prevent blood clots. These compounds are more potent in raw onions.

- The potassium in bananas is thought to help reduce plaque formation in arteries.

Asparagus contains a flavonoid called rutin. This works with vitamin C to strengthen capillary walls.

Mushrooms, particularly strong-tasting varieties such as shitake, help reduce blood pressure and LDL-cholesterol levels. Cooking them does not reduce any of their health benefits.

Mediterranean Tart

Use this concept for other seasonal vegetables such as asparagus and mushrooms.

> 3 red capsicums
> 3 yellow capsicums
> 12 slices omega-3 enriched wholegrain bread
> avocado or olive oil spray
> ¼ cup sun-dried tomato pesto
> 2 egg whites
> ½ teaspoon prepared minced chilli
> Parmesan cheese shavings
> fresh basil leaves

Cut capsicums in half and remove seeds. Place on an oven tray and grill until skins are blistered and black. Remove from oven. When cool enough to handle, peel off skins and cut into thirds. Remove crusts from bread. (Discard or make into soft breadcrumbs for later.) Spray slices with oil spray. With oil side out, line the base and sides of a 20cm round springform tin, overlapping the bread slices as necessary. Bake at 160°C for 45 minutes or until bread is crisp. Spread base of bread case with tomato pesto. Arrange the capsicum slices over the pesto. Lightly beat egg whites and chilli together to break up the egg white. Pour over capsicums. Bake at 180°C for 45 minutes or until egg is set. Scatter Parmesan cheese shavings over and garnish with basil leaves.

Serves 6

Mexican Beef Tortillas with Avocado Salsa

Just because you are looking after your heart doesn't mean red meat must be banished. It is still the best source of readily absorbed iron and zinc.

> 1 red onion
> 2 cloves garlic
> 100g piece rump steak
> 1 carrot
> 425g can Mexican-style chilli beans
> 140g pot tomato paste
> ½ cup red wine
> 10 corn tortillas

Peel onion and chop finely. Crush, peel and chop garlic. Trim any fat from steak. Slice meat thinly. Scrub carrot and grate. Heat a non-stick frying pan over medium heat and dry fry the onion and garlic for 3 to 4 minutes. Add steak slices and quickly stir fry. Remove meat from pan and add chilli beans, tomato paste and red wine. Bring to the boil then mix in meat. Place some mixture down the centre of each tortilla. Top with grated carrot. Fold tortilla over to cover filling. Place seam-side down on an oven tray. Bake at 200°C for 10 minutes or until lightly golden. Serve cut in half with Avocado Salsa.

Avocado Salsa

> 1 medium tomato
> ½ ripe avocado
> 1 stick celery
> 2 tablespoons lemon juice
> freshly ground black pepper

Cut tomato into 1cm cubes, removing core. Peel and destone avocado. Chop flesh into cubes. Trim celery and chop finely. Mix tomato, avocado, celery and lemon juice together. Grind black pepper over.

Serves 4

- The lycopene in tomatoes protects hearts and lungs from the damage caused by free radicals.

- Corn offers us plenty of the B vitamin niacin, which helps regulate cholesterol in the blood.

- Fish that have medium levels of oil include bluenose, brill, blue cod, John Dory, piper, hapuka, hake, ling, monkfish, deep-sea cod, terakihi and school shark.

- Hoki and snapper have medium-to-low levels of fish oil.

- Fish with low oil content include red cod, flounder, gurnard, sole, trevally and whitebait.

- Fish oils help lower cholesterol levels and high blood-pressure, protecting the heart against disease and generally strengthening the cardiovascular system.

Steamed Fish Rolls with Sweet Chilli Sauce

250g fillet skinned and boned salmon, cod, tuna, marlin or other medium-to-high oil-content fish
2 spring onions
2 tablespoons low-salt soy sauce
2 tablespoons lime juice
½ teaspoon prepared minced chilli
1 tablespoon chopped fresh coriander
4 x 21cm round rice paper sheets
chives

Wash and dry fish. Cut into 2cm cubes. Trim spring onions and slice thinly. Place fish and spring onions in a bowl with soy sauce, lime juice, chilli and coriander. Mix to combine. Soak rice papers in hot water for 1 minute or until just softened. Place on a board in a single layer. Divide fish mixture evenly among sheets, placing down the centre of the sheet. Fold and roll sheets to enclose mixture. Tie with a chive. Place in a lightly oiled steamer and steam, covered, over boiling water for 4 minutes. Serve with steamed bok choy or spinach and sweet chilli sauce.

Serves 2

important ingredients to improve cholesterol levels

olive oil
sesame oil
safflower oil
sunflower oil
walnut oil
tuna
salmon
sardines
anchovies
kahawai
peanuts
peanut butter
cashew nuts
almonds
apples

pears
bananas
oranges
mandarins
grapefruit
sweet cherries
cranberries
avocados
raisins
beans
lentils
chickpeas
kidney beans
carrots
celery

artichokes
cauliflower
peas
Brussels sprouts
alfalfa sprouts
onions
garlic
oats
oat bran
soya beans
soy milk
tofu
tempeh
miso

the real oil

If there is one thing to put a quiver in the liver, it is the mention of cholesterol. Over the years, fear and confusion have become synonymous with cholesterol. My need to deconfuse the issue, without having to go to med school, justifies a separate chapter for this important topic.

When you have a cholesterol test you get three results: an HDL, an LDL and an overall cholesterol reading. HDL (high-density lipoprotein) cholesterol is the good cholesterol. LDL (low-density lipoprotein) cholesterol is the bad cholesterol. I remember this by calling it the lousy cholesterol. The ratio of the HDL to the LDL cholesterol gives the overall cholesterol reading.

If your LDL level is much higher than your HDL level, you have a problem. Changes in your diet can help lower your LDL cholesterol levels, thereby looking after your heart-health. If your diet relies heavily on animal and saturated plant fats and trans-fats, your LDL level will be high. Don't forget though that good cholesterol is essential for good health and our livers make cholesterol.

Raised cholesterol is usually easily controlled by diet for most people. However, if your body is overzealous in its production of cholesterol, medication may be your only option.

Warm Winter Salad with Orange and Walnut Vinaigrette

If you don't like walnuts, change the oil and nuts. Try peanuts, almonds or cashews and olive or avocado oil.

    10 Brussels sprouts
    1 large carrot
    1 red onion
    2 sticks celery
    ½ cup walnuts

Trim Brussels sprouts. Cut a cross in the stem. Scrub carrot, trim ends and cut into matchstick pieces. Steam Brussels sprouts over boiling water for 5 minutes. Add carrot and steam for a further 3 minutes. Remove from heat. Cut Brussels sprouts into quarters and place in a bowl with carrots. Peel onion, cut in half and slice thinly. Trim celery and cut into 1cm pieces on the diagonal. Add onion, celery and walnuts to sprouts. Pour Orange and Walnut Vinaigrette over. Toss to coat.

Orange and Walnut Vinaigrette

    ¼ cup walnut oil
    1 tablespoon tarragon vinegar
    2 tablespoons orange juice
    ½ teaspoon grated orange rind

Mix walnut oil, tarragon vinegar, orange juice and orange rind together.

Serves 4

- Safflower, sunflower and walnut oils are all polyunsaturated oils, good for keeping that ratio of HDL to LDL cholesterol in check.

- Research has shown that a raw onion a day can improve the ratio of HDL cholesterol and LDL cholesterol in your body, by increasing the level of HDL.

- Globe artichokes contain a compound that increases the production of bile by the liver. Bile helps the body remove cholesterol. Research has shown artichokes can lower levels of LDL cholesterol, thereby giving a better ratio of good to bad cholesterols in the blood.

- Monounsaturated fats include olive oil. These fats increase the level of HDL cholesterol in the body.

Artichoke Pasta with Lemon and Capers

1 onion
2 cloves garlic
1 red capsicum
1 tablespoon olive oil
1 lemon
390g can artichoke hearts
50g snow peas
2 tablespoons drained capers
3 cups cooked drained pasta
soy or Parmesan cheese

Peel onion and chop finely. Crush, peel and chop garlic. Cut capsicum in half. Remove seeds and cut flesh into 1cm cubes. Heat oil in a frying pan and sauté onion, garlic and capsicum over a medium heat until soft. Grate rind from lemon and squeeze juice. Drain artichokes, reserving ½ cup of brine. Cut artichoke hearts into quarters. String snow peas and cut in half lengthwise. Add to pan with lemon juice, rind, capers and reserved brine. Bring to the boil. Toss mixture through hot cooked pasta. Serve garnished with grated soy or Parmesan cheese.

Serves 3

important ingredients to ease menopause

kidney beans
haricot beans
lima beans
cannellini beans
lentils
chickpeas
berries
nuts
soya beans
soy milk
tofu
tempeh

miso
yams
sweet potatoes (kumara)
broccoli
peas
beetroot
carrots
celery
garlic
sage
flaxseed oil
linseed oil

sesame seeds
pumpkin seeds
poppy seeds
caraway seeds
sunflower seeds
tuna
salmon
sardines
anchovies
kahawai

freedom fighting

Menopause has to be a misnomer — there is nothing too pausing about this time in a woman's or, for that matter, a man's life. Yes, men too experience menopause, albeit not as dramatically as some women.

Whilst diet may not solve all the problems of menopause, taking control of your food choices can have a major impact on the extent of the symptoms. It means making a shift in your awareness of what you eat and a conscious effort to choose foods that will benefit you at this exciting time of life.

Soy products probably make the major contribution to controlling menopause symptoms. When I discovered I had a dairy allergy I had no choice but to move my flat white from milk to soy. It is, however, a flavour you get used to, especially when you know that it is doing a good turn for your body. Foods you might not have considered before can be easily incorporated and, if necessary, disguised for those of us who don't like eating chunks of tofu or tempeh.

However, if you are already on the menopause roller coaster do not expect a miraculous change overnight. Change happens gradually so, if possible, it is best to adjust your diet before the onset of menopause to maximise the effect of diet on your body as it fights for the freedom it so rightly deserves.

Simple Sweet Rollups

These are delicious served warm for a weekend breakfast after a bowl of oatmeal. I use soy milk all the time for my baking, usually substituting half milk and half water for a milk measure. Try making these in the food processor. It is so easy.

1 cup flour
1 cup wholemeal flour
4 teaspoons baking powder
1 tablespoon sugar
50g butter or ¼ cup flaxseed oil or ¼ cup olive oil
¾ cup low-fat soy milk

Mix flours and baking powder in a bowl. Mix in sugar. Melt butter and mix into dry ingredients or mix in oil. Using a fork (or in a food processor) mix in enough soy milk to make a stiff dough. Gather into a ball and roll out on a lightly floured board to form a 27 x 17cm rectangle. Spread filling over dough to within 1cm of edges. Roll up from the long side Swiss-roll style. Cut dough into 2cm slices. Place on baking tray and bake at 200°C for 8 to 10 minutes or until cooked and lightly golden.

Filling

1 cup chopped dried fruit such as dates, prunes, apricots
¼ cup chopped nuts such as pecans, walnuts, almonds
1 teaspoon mixed spice
3 tablespoons runny honey or maple syrup

Mix dried fruit, nuts, mixed spice and honey or maple syrup together.

Makes 9

- Linseed, also known as flaxseed, contains omega-3 fatty acids. It also contains lignans, which are phytoestrogens. These lignans alter the balance of oestrogen in the body so don't overdose on the linseed. Two to three tablespoons a day is enough as the husks are toxic in high doses.

- Replace tea, coffee and sweetened fizzy drinks with herbal or fruit teas, sugar-free juices, cordials and water. Fruit-based drinks make a good substitute on alcohol-free days.

- Oats help stabilise oestrogen levels and reduce water retention.

There is always a concern about reduced bone density after menopause. Knowing that the calcium from animal sources is rapidly absorbed but more easily lost from the body is important. That is why vegetable sources of calcium become more important. Although they are less easily absorbed they are retained longer.

Sage is thought to help reduce hot flushes. Try using it to make a fresh herb tea.

Kumara, Pumpkin and Split Pea Soup with Sesame Sage Pesto

2 onions
4 cloves garlic
500g piece pumpkin
1 kumara
1 tablespoon olive oil
2 tablespoons miso paste
2 cups cold water
1 cup yellow split peas
4 cups cold vegetable or chicken stock

Peel onions and chop finely. Crush, peel and chop garlic. Peel pumpkin and deseed. Cut into chunks. Peel kumara and cut into chunks. Heat oil in a large saucepan. Sauté onion and garlic for 5 minutes or until clear. Stir miso paste into water. Add pumpkin, kumara, split peas, stock and miso to the saucepan. Cover and bring to the boil. Simmer for 30 to 40 minutes or until vegetables are soft and peas tender. Mash to break up pumpkin and kumara. Serve hot garnished with Sesame Sage Pesto.

Sesame Sage Pesto

1 cup sage leaves
¼ cup safflower oil
1 tablespoon sesame oil
2 teaspoons toasted sesame seeds

Place sage leaves in a food processor. Process to chop. Add oils and sesame seeds and process until combined but still coarse.

Makes ¼ cup

Serves 6

Savoury Tarte Tatin

1 large kumara
1 cup flour
2 teaspoons baking powder
fresh sage

Peel kumara and cut into chunks. Cook in boiling water for 10 minutes or until soft. Reserve ½ cup cooking water. Mash kumara in cooking water and leave to cool. Mix in flour and baking powder to form a stiff, manageable dough, adding more flour if necessary. Wrap in plastic wrap and refrigerate while preparing the topping. Roll or press dough out to size of pan used for topping on a piece of baking paper. Carefully lift to cover topping mixture in pan. Return to heat and cook over a medium heat for 10 minutes. Place pan under a hot grill and cook kumara base until golden. Run a knife around edge of pan to loosen tatin and turn onto a serving plate. Serve garnished with fresh sage.

Topping

6 shallots
8 cloves garlic
250g tofu
2 medium-sized fresh beetroot
1 tablespoon olive oil
2 tablespoons capsicum relish
1 tablespoon hot water

Peel shallots and cut into halves. Peel garlic, leaving cloves whole. Cut tofu into 1cm wide chip shapes. Trim beetroot and peel. Cut into 1cm wedges. Heat olive oil in a 24cm frying pan with an ovenproof handle. Sauté onion, garlic and beetroot over a medium heat for 5 minutes. Remove from heat. Spread evenly over base of pan and arrange tofu on top. Mix capsicum relish and water together and pour over mixture in pan.

Serves 4

Beetroot is a powerful antioxidant and detoxifier and is therefore a beneficial food to include before and during menopause to help alleviate its symptoms.

Tofu contains large quantities of calcium thanks to the calcium compounds used in its processing. Calcium is important for maintaining healthy bones, particularly after menopause.

Carrot and Poppy Seed Salad

2 carrots
1 tablespoon poppy seeds
2 tablespoons chopped parsley
1 lemon

Scrub carrots and grate. Mix carrot, poppy seeds and parsley together. Squeeze over the juice from the lemon and toss to coat.

- Broccoli and carrots seem to have a major impact on the health of just about every organ in the body. They have a powerful cleansing effect on the liver, which is the major detoxifying organ in the body. Use carrots as a snack in a pre- and during-menopause regime for a healthy liver and good sustained energy supply.

- Phytoestrogens (oestrogens from plants) improve moistening, cooling and lubricating functions in the body, helping to alleviate hot flushes and keep other important body functions fully operational.

- Bananas contain vitamin B6, which may help alleviate menopause-related problems. They help to produce amino acids that control mood. Broccoli, kidney beans and bananas are also good sources of vitamin B6.

Middle Eastern Broccoli Crustless Quiche with Carrot and Poppy Seed Salad

2 onions
2 cloves garlic
1 head broccoli
4 eggs
¼ cup hummus
½ cup flour
1 cup low-fat soy milk
½ cup water
1 teaspoon prepared minced chilli
½ teaspoon salt
freshly ground black pepper
2 tablespoons pine nuts or chopped walnuts

Peel onions and chop finely. Crush, peel and chop garlic. Dry fry onion and garlic in a non-stick pan for 5 minutes or until onion is clear. Wash broccoli and cut into florets. Place eggs, hummus, flour, soy milk, water, chilli, salt, pepper and broccoli florets into the bowl of a food processor and process until combined and broccoli is coarsely chopped. Mix in onion and garlic. Alternatively chop broccoli coarsely and beat ingredients with a whisk instead of using a food processor. Pour mixture into a 20cm quiche dish. Sprinkle with nuts. Bake at 180°C for 45 minutes or until mixture is set. Serve hot or cold with Carrot and Poppy Seed Salad.

Serves 6

Warm Soba Noodle Lamb and Steamed Vegetable Salad with Sesame Ginger Dressing

2 lamb fillets or 200g lean boneless lamb
100g snow peas
300g asparagus
2 cloves garlic
3 spring onions
4 large brown mushrooms
1 teaspoon sesame oil
125g soba noodles
snow pea sprouts

Trim any fat or sinew from lamb fillets. Trim and string snow peas. Break tough ends from asparagus and trim to neaten. Cut spears in half on the diagonal. Crush, peel and chop garlic. Trim spring onions and cut into 1cm slices on the diagonal. Wipe mushrooms and slice. Heat sesame oil in a frying pan and sauté garlic and spring onions for 2 minutes. Add mushrooms and stir-fry for 1 minute. Remove from heat. Grill lamb fillets for 1 to 2 minutes or until still pink in the middle. Rest for 5 minutes. Place asparagus and snow peas in a steamer and cook over boiling water for 3 to 5 minutes. Cook noodles in boiling water for 3 minutes or to packet instructions. Drain well. Divide among four serving bowls. Cut lamb into 0.5cm thick slices. Toss lamb, vegetables, mushroom mixture and Sesame Ginger Dressing together and serve over noodles. Garnish with snow pea sprouts.

Sesame Ginger Dressing

2 tablespoons grated fresh ginger
2 tablespoons tahini
1 tablespoon flaxseed oil or olive oil
¼ cup white vinegar
3 tablespoons soy sauce

Place ginger, tahini, oil, vinegar and soy sauce in a screw-top jar. Shake to combine.

Serves 4

* Wherever there is fat in an animal food there is oestrogen. Removing as much animal fat as possible from our diet will reduce the influence of these unwanted oestrogens.

* Yams help stabilise oestrogen levels and help mood swings and other menopause-related problems.

- An imbalance in hormones will accentuate menopause symptoms. Diet can play a significant part in helping balance hormone levels.

- Oily fish, such as tuna and salmon, feature heavily in all aspects of anti-aging health.

Japanese-style Fish Kebabs

400g piece fresh tuna, salmon or other oily fish
3 cloves garlic
1 tablespoon finely grated fresh ginger
2 tablespoons red miso paste
¼ teaspoon smoked paprika
¼ cup mirin
2 sticks celery
120g mesclun
1 sheet toasted nori
1 teaspoon sesame oil
2 tablespoons mirin
2 tablespoons Japanese-style pickled ginger

Cut fish into 2cm cubes and place in a shallow dish. Crush, peel and finely chop garlic. Mix garlic, ginger, miso, paprika and first measure of mirin together. Pour over fish. Set aside for 15 to 20 minutes. Thread fish onto eight skewers or bamboo satay sticks. Trim celery and cut into thin sticks on the diagonal. Wash and dry mesclun. Shred nori finely. Toss celery and nori through mesclun. Cook kebabs for 2 minutes or until just cooked. Arrange mesclun on serving plates. Mix sesame oil, second measure of mirin and any residual marinade together. Place kebabs on top of mesclun, drizzle with sesame oil mixture and serve with pickled ginger.

Serves 4

Stir-fried Vietnamese Beef

Having the steak partly frozen makes it easier to slice thinly.

1 onion
2 cloves garlic
300g piece topside or rump steak
1 red capsicum
1 head broccoli
2 stalks celery
4cm long piece fresh ginger
1 carrot
1 tablespoon peanut oil
1 teaspoon sesame oil
¼ cup black bean sauce
¼ cup water
1 cup fresh mint leaves
½ cup fresh coriander leaves

Peel onion and cut into rings. Crush, peel and chop garlic. Thinly slice topside or rump steak. Cut capsicum in half. Remove seeds and cut flesh into thin strips. Wash broccoli and cut into florets. Trim celery and cut into thin strips. Peel ginger and cut into thin strips. Scrub carrot and grate coarsely. Heat oils in a wok or large frying pan. Sauté onion and garlic for 2 to 3 minutes. Stir-fry meat in batches for 30 seconds to 1 minute or until almost cooked. Remove each batch from wok or pan and set aside. Add broccoli to wok. Stir-fry one minute. Add capsicum, celery and ginger and stir-fry for 2 minutes. Return meat to pan and mix in black bean sauce and water. Bring to the boil. Toss through carrot, mint and coriander leaves and serve with steamed rice.

Serves 4

Three servings of broccoli a week can be beneficial for people suffering depression. The folic acid in broccoli promotes the production of serotonin. This is a mood-lifting chemical that is found at only low levels in people suffering from depression. Depression and mood swings can be a side effect of menopause.

Fats in the diet are essential because they make up many necessary parts of our bodies. These include hormones and nerve coverings.

- Soy products, chickpeas, dried beans and lentils are all rich in phytoestrogens.

- Our bodies have oestrogen receptors onto which oestrogen attaches. At menopause, when oestrogen levels change, many of these receptors can fill up with oestrogen, if there is an oversupply, or they are left unfilled, if there is an undersupply. Either way, the effect is dramatic. The best way to overcome this problem is to make changes in your diet, preferably before menopause, to include foods that contain phytoestrogens.

- Phytoestrogens are about 100 times weaker than other oestrogens, yet they are taken up by the oestrogen receptors helping to keep the body in oestrogen balance. A diet rich in phytoestrogens for men and women is the best way to avoid the nasty side affects of menopause.

Delicious White Bean Mash

Use haricot beans for this if you have time to cook from scratch. Soak the beans for a couple of hours. Drain and cook with plenty of stock and the other flavourings for 40 to 45 minutes or until tender. If using canned beans, check the list of ingredients – you do not want beans with added sugar or salt.

1 onion
2 cloves garlic
1 cup vegetable stock
1 bay leaf
2 sprigs sage
2 sticks celery with tops on
300g can white butter beans
avocado oil

Peel onion and chop finely. Crush, peel and chop garlic. Place onion, garlic, stock, bay leaf, sage and celery stalks in a saucepan. Cover and bring to the boil. Reduce heat and simmer for 5 minutes. Add beans and simmer for 5 minutes. Remove bay, sage and celery and discard. Mash beans with a potato masher. Serve drizzled with a little avocado oil as a vegetable accompaniment.

Serves 2

New York Cheesecake

Chances are your friends are at the same stage in life as you so why not look after everyone's wellbeing when entertaining? I'm not big on eating chunks of tofu but this is an excellent way to gain the advantages of eating soy without compromising texture or taste, and it will impress at your next dinner party.

Base

14 digestive biscuits
½ cup blanched almonds or ground almonds
50g butter

Filling

500g soft curd tofu
½ cup sugar
2 tablespoons lemon juice
2 tablespoons grated lemon rind
4 eggs
1 teaspoon vanilla essence
1 cup low-fat soy milk

Place biscuits and almonds in the bowl of a food processor and process until fine crumbs. Alternatively, crush biscuits and mix with ground almonds. Melt butter and mix into crumb mixture until combined. Press into the base of a 20cm springform tin. Place tofu in the bowl of a food processor and process until smooth. Add sugar, lemon juice, rind, eggs, vanilla and soy milk. Process until combined. Alternatively, sieve tofu and beat with remaining ingredients until smooth. Pour filling over base and bake at 160°C for 1 hour and 15 minutes or until set. Turn oven off but leave cheesecake in oven for a further 15 minutes. Remove from oven and allow to cool. Serve with a Raspberry Coulis and fresh berries.

Raspberry Coulis

2 cups fresh or frozen raspberries
2 tablespoons icing sugar

Process, blend or sieve raspberries. Sieve purée to remove seeds if using a processor or blender. Mix in icing sugar to taste.

Serves 8 to 10

important ingredients for a healthy prostate

sunflower seeds
sesame seeds
pumpkin seeds
Brazil nuts
tomatoes
cabbage
mushrooms
onions
Brussels sprouts

broccoli
bok choy
cauliflower
watermelon
pink grapefruit
guava
papaya
apricots
cranberries

apples
oysters
mussels
soya beans
soy milk
tofu
tempeh
miso

little jack horner

After what sometimes seems a life sentence being a woman, there is always a slight satisfaction when the men in our lives have to go and have their prostate checked.

There was a worldwide hurricane when all the men sighed with relief at the introduction of a blood test for checking prostate health. Sorry, boys, but it has been found to be unreliable. The digital method is still the most reliable way to check prostate function. (I think that must have been decided by a woman.) It is good to take preventative measures to ensure those tests always return a negative result.

It is so easy to incorporate foods in an everyday diet that will give a man the best shot at maintaining a healthy prostate. So, fellas, take a grip on yourselves and make sure you, or whoever makes the food choices in your household, incorporate foods for prostate protection on a regular basis. And girls, just remember we have a vested interest in this too!

Steamed Greens with Seedy Sprinkle

1 head broccoli
3 stalks celery
1 bunch spinach
8 small Brussels sprouts

Wash broccoli and cut into florets. Trim celery and cut into serving-sized pieces. Wash spinach and trim stalks. Trim Brussels sprouts. Place broccoli in a steamer and cook over boiling water for 5 minutes. Add celery and Brussels sprouts to steamer and cook for 3 minutes. Add spinach and cook for 1 minute. Remove from steamer and toss vegetables together. Sprinkle over 2 tablespoons Seedy Sprinkle and serve.

Serves 6

Seedy Sprinkle or Dukkah Dipper

¼ cup poppy seeds
2 tablespoons linseed
2 tablespoons sesame seeds
2 tablespoons pumpkin seeds
1 tablespoon fennel seeds
1 teaspoon ground cumin
1 teaspoon ground coriander
1 teaspoon grated lemon rind

Place all the seeds in a food processor or clean coffee grinder and process until crushed. This makes the nutrients stored in the seeds able to be used by the body. Mix in cumin, coriander and lemon rind. Store in an airtight container in the fridge.

Makes ¾ cup

- Pumpkin seeds contain B vitamins, calcium, iron, magnesium and zinc, all of which help prostate health.

- Sesame seeds contain high levels of vitamin E, folic acid, calcium, selenium, iron, magnesium and zinc.

Eating raw tomatoes is not the secret to increasing the lycopene levels in your body. Cooking tomatoes, especially with a little oil, helps release the lycopene from the fibres of the cell walls in the tomato. Lycopene is fat soluble so adding a little oil in the cooking process helps transport the lycopene, making it available to the body.

In some European countries, pumpkin seeds have been used as a remedy for benign enlargement of the prostate.

Moroccan Chicken Casserole

2 onions
4 cloves garlic
1 tablespoon avocado oil
1 cup red lentils
6 skinned and boned chicken thighs
140g pot tomato paste
400g can Moroccan-style tomatoes
2 cups chicken stock
½ cup pitted prunes
½ cup dried apricots
2 tablespoons chopped parsley
3 tablespoons chopped pumpkin seeds

Peel onions and chop finely. Crush, peel and chop garlic. Heat oil in a pan and sauté onion and garlic over medium heat for 5 minutes. Wash lentils. Place in the bottom of a 10-cup capacity casserole dish. Place chicken on top, making sure all fat is removed. Add tomato paste and onion to Moroccan tomatoes. Mix to combine. Pour chicken stock into casserole then pour over tomato mixture. Cover and cook at 180°C for 1 hour. Add prunes and apricots. Cover and cook for a further 40 minutes. Mix parsley and pumpkin seeds together. Sprinkle over casserole and serve.

Serves 6

Steamed Fish Parcels with Bok Choy and Oyster Sauce

If you have individual bamboo steamer baskets, use these instead of wrapping the fish in paper.

    2 fillets white-fleshed, skinned and boned fish
    2 small heads bok choy
    1 stick celery
    2 spring onions
    2 large brown mushrooms
    2 tablespoons oyster sauce

Wash and dry fish and cut into 2cm-wide crosswise strips. Wash bok choy, trim and cut in half lengthwise. Place each bok choy in the centre of a piece of baking paper. Divide fish pieces, placing half on top of each bok choy. Trim celery and cut into 2cm-long pieces on the diagonal. Trim spring onions, cut in half and cut into thin lengthwise strips. Trim mushrooms and slice thinly. Place half the celery, spring onions and mushrooms on top of each parcel. Spoon half the oyster sauce over each mixture. Wrap paper around fish mixture into a tight package. Place on a rack over a pan of boiling water. Cover and steam for 5 minutes or until fish is cooked. To serve, cut paper in a cross shape to reveal contents. Serve with steamed brown or white rice. If using bamboo steamers, cover with the lid and steam over boiling water in a wok or frying pan.

Serves 2

- Fish is one of the better sources of selenium, which helps protect against prostate cancer. Selenium attacks free radicals.

- Mushrooms are a good source of selenium (among other things) and are therefore good for prostate-health.

When cooking vegetables, always put them into boiling, unsalted water or, better still, steam them to retain as many nutrients as possible. A little water and short cooking times will give you the most nutrients from your vegetables if you must boil them. Adding salt to the cooking water leaches out valuable nutrients during cooking by drawing water from the vegetables. Use salt sparingly and add after cooking if you must.

Vegetable Curry

¼ cauliflower
1 head broccoli
8 Brussels sprouts
12 asparagus spears or green beans
200g piece pumpkin
2 onions
4 cloves garlic
1 tablespoon avocado oil
1 tablespoon hot curry powder
2 x 400g can Indian-style tomatoes
2 cups vegetable stock
2 tablespoons tomato paste
1 teaspoon salt
1 tablespoon chopped fresh coriander

Wash cauliflower and broccoli and cut into florets. Cut Brussels sprouts in half. Break woody ends from asparagus and cut spears in half. If using beans, top and tail, string and cut in half. Peel and deseed pumpkin. Cut into cubes. Peel onions and cut into 0.5cm slices. Crush, peel and chop garlic. Heat avocado oil in a saucepan large enough to cook all the vegetables. Sauté onion and garlic over medium heat for 5 minutes. Add curry powder and cook for 1 minute or until spices smell fragrant. Add tomatoes, vegetable stock, tomato paste and salt to saucepan and bring to the boil. Add pumpkin and cook for 5 minutes. Add cauliflower, broccoli, Brussels sprouts and asparagus or beans and cook for 10 to 15 minutes or until vegetables are tender. Serve hot, garnished with coriander.

Serves 6

Fruit Betty

Leftovers, if you are lucky enough to have any, are great for breakfast.

> ½ cup dried apricots
> ½ cup boiling water
> 3 apples
> 410g can guavas
> ½ cup dried cranberries
> 2 teaspoons grated lemon rind
> 2 cups wholegrain breadcrumbs
> ¼ cup brown sugar
> ¼ cup chopped Brazil nuts

Put apricots in a bowl. Pour over boiling water and set aside while preparing remaining ingredients. Cut apples into quarters, remove cores and cut each quarter into five slices. Arrange in an 8-cup capacity ovenproof dish or six 1-cup capacity ovenproof dishes. Drain guavas (use juice for something else) and cut in half if large. Arrange over apples. Place undrained apricots in dish with fruit. Sprinkle over cranberries. Mix lemon rind, breadcrumbs, sugar and Brazil nuts together. Sprinkle crumb mixture over fruit. Bake at 180°C for 35 minutes or until apples are soft and crumbs are lightly golden.

Serves 6

- Brazil nuts are rich in selenium. High intakes of selenium have been linked to low rates of prostate cancer.

- It only takes one Brazil nut to get all the selenium you need for a day.

Spiced Nuts
To Serve with Drinks

1 cup Brazil nuts
1 cup hazelnuts
1 cup blanched almonds
1 cup cashew nuts
1 cup pecans
4 tablespoons Thai red curry paste
1 sheet toasted nori

Put nuts in a bowl. Add curry paste and toss nuts to coat evenly. Turn into a roasting dish and roast nuts at 180°C for 15 to 20 minutes or until nuts are lightly golden. Cool. Roll nori tightly. Cut down the centre lengthwise. Stack nori pieces and shred finely. Mix through nuts. Store in an airtight container until ready to serve.

Makes 5 cups

> The phytoestrogens in soy products help protect against hormone-related cancers such as prostate cancer.

Avocado and Smoked Salmon Pâté
To Serve with Drinks

1 clove garlic
1 avocado
100g smoked salmon pieces
125g tofu
1 tablespoon tomato paste
½ teaspoon prepared minced chilli
1 small tomato
1 tablespoon chopped parsley
wholegrain toast

Crush and peel garlic. Peel and destone avocado. Chop flesh roughly. Place garlic, avocado, salmon, tofu, tomato paste and chilli in a food processor or blender and process until smooth. Pile into a dish. Finely chop tomato. Mix with parsley. Place on pâté. Serve with wholegrain toast.

Makes 1½ cups

index

alfalfa sprouts
    health benefits, 105
    Sunday Night Pizza, 104, 105
almonds
    Almond and Oatmeal Hotcakes with Honeyed Bananas, 30, 31
    Almond Apple Cake with Apple Sauce, 66, 67
    health benefits, 72
    Italian Honey Nut Panforte, 46, 47
    My Magnificent Quick Muesli, 92, 93
    Skinful for Breakfast, 50, 51
    Sweet Raisin Treats, 110, 111
anchovy and wasabi mayo, 21
apples
    Almond Apple Cake with Apple Sauce, 66, 67
    health benefits, 31, 67
    Pear and Apple Nut Crumble, 108, 109
artichokes, globe
    Artichoke Pasta with Lemon and Capers, 102, 103
    health benefits, 102
asparagus, health benefits, 80
avocados
    Avocado and Smoked Salmon Pâté, 148, 149
    Avocado Skin-tonic Salad with Roasted Capsicum Vinaigrette, 54, 55
    Fresh Pineapple Salsa for Chicken or Fish, 42, 43
    health benefits, 43, 55
    Mexican Beef Tortillas with Avocado Salsa, 82, 83
    Salmon Puffs with Chopped Egg and Avocado, 40, 41
    Smoked Salmon, Avocado and Cucumber Salad, 98, 99

bananas
    Almond and Oatmeal Hotcakes with Honeyed Bananas, 30, 31
    Banana and Cracked Wheat Muffins, 44, 45
    Carrot, Orange and Banana Semolina Cake, 106, 107
    Curried Kumara, Banana and Broccoli Salad, 78, 79
    health benefits, 32, 36, 71, 79, 120
    Tarzan's Joint Juice, 32, 33
beans, dried, 39
    Delicious White Bean Mash, 128, 129
    health benefits, 39, 128
    Mexican Beef Tortillas with Avocado Salsa, 82, 83
    Sunday Night Pizza, 104, 105
beef
    Mexican Beef Tortillas with Avocado Salsa, 82, 83
    Stir-fried Vietnamese Beef, 126, 127
beetroot
    Beetroot, Spinach and Broccoli Salad, 10, 11
    health benefits, 10, 87, 119
    Savoury Tarte Tatin, 118, 119
berries – see also specific berries, e.g. blueberries
    Fresh Berry Terrine, 24, 25
    health benefits, 9, 51
    Very Berry Sorbet, 22, 23
blueberries
    health benefits, 9, 22, 25, 31, 51
    Mocha Dessert Cake with Fresh Blueberry Sauce, 26, 27
    Straw-Blue Fruit Smoothie, 8, 9

bok choy and oyster sauce, steamed fish parcels with, 142, 143
Brazil nuts
    Fruit Betty, 146, 147
    health benefits, 147
    Skinful for Breakfast, 50, 51
broccoli
    Beetroot, Spinach and Broccoli Salad, 10, 11
    Curried Kumara, Banana and Broccoli Salad, 78, 79
    health benefits, 13, 36, 79, 120, 127, 136
    Middle Eastern Broccoli Crustless Quiche with Carrot and Poppy Seed Salad, 120, 121
Brussels sprouts
    health benefits, 144
    Warm Winter Salad with Orange and Walnut Vinaigrette, 100, 101

cabbage
    Green Goddess and Garlic Soup, 36, 37
    health benefits, 36, 136
    Jack's Slaw, 136, 137
capsicums
    Avocado Skin-tonic Salad with Roasted Capsicum Vinaigrette, 54, 55
    health benefits, 55
    Mediterranean Tart, 80, 81
    Roasted Tomato, Carrot and Capsicum Soup, 134, 135
carrots
    Carrot and Lentil Soup, 94, 95
    Carrot and Poppy Seed Salad, 120, 121
    Carrot, Orange and Banana Semolina Cake, 106, 107
    health benefits, 13, 59, 94
    Roasted Tomato, Carrot and Capsicum Soup, 134, 135
    Sardine Lunch Toasties, 76, 77
    Steamed Mussels with Thai Spices, 58, 59
    Warm Winter Salad with Orange and Walnut Vinaigrette, 101
cauliflower, health benefits, 144
chicken
    Chicken and Vegetable Soup, 12, 13
    Fresh Pineapple Salsa for Chicken or Fish, 42, 43
    health benefits, 36
    Indian Chicken and Mango Stir-fry, 62, 63
    Moroccan Chicken Casserole, 140, 141
chickpeas, health benefits, 128
chillies
    Fresh Pineapple Salsa for Chicken or Fish, 42, 43
    health benefits, 43
    Steamed Fish Rolls with Sweet Chilli Sauce, 84, 85
chocolate
    health benefits, 26
    Mocha Dessert Cake with Fresh Blueberry Sauce, 26, 27
coffee
    health benefits, 26
    Mocha Dessert Cake with Fresh Blueberry Sauce, 26, 27
corn
    health benefits, 83
    Mexican Beef Tortillas with Avocado Salsa, 82, 83
cracked wheat and banana muffins, 44, 45
cranberries
    Carrot, Orange and Banana Semolina Cake, 106, 107
    Fresh Berry Terrine, 24, 25
    health benefits, 71, 93
    My Magnificent Quick Muesli, 92, 93
    Tarzan's Joint Juice, 32, 33
cucumber, salad of smoked salmon, avocado and, 98, 99

Date, Prune and Rhubarb Loaf, 88, 89
Dukkah Dipper, 138, 139

eggplant, health benefits, 97
eggs
    Middle Eastern Broccoli Crustless Quiche with Carrot and Poppy Seed Salad, 120, 121
    Salmon Puffs with Chopped Egg and Avocado, 40, 41
    Smoked Salmon, Spinach and Egg Pies, 16, 17

fish – see also salmon; seafood; tuna
    Asian Seafood and Rice Noodle Soup, 34, 35
    Favourite Fish with Lime Mint and Mango Salsa, 64, 65
    Fresh Pineapple Salsa for Chicken or Fish, 42, 43
    health benefits, 14, 17, 21, 35, 40, 56, 84, 143
    Japanese Style Fish Kebabs, 124, 125
    oil content, 21, 84
    Sardine Lunch Toasties, 76, 77
    Steamed Fish Parcels with Bok Choy and Oyster Sauce, 142, 143
    Steamed Fish Rolls with Sweet Chilli Sauce, 84, 85
fruit – see also specific fruits, e.g. blueberries
    Fruit Betty, 146, 147
    health benefits, 25, 60, 97
    Simple Sweet Rollups, 114, 115
    Toasted Breakfast Muffins with Fresh Fruit, 70, 71
    Winter Fruit Salad, 72, 73

garlic
    Green Goddess and Garlic Soup, 36, 37
    health benefits, 64, 75, 79, 94
ginger
    Asian Seafood and Rice Noodle Soup, 34, 35
    Fresh Pineapple Salsa for Chicken or Fish, 42, 43
    health benefits, 35, 39
    Salmon and Noodle Salad, 56
    Sesame Ginger Dressing, 123
gout, foods to avoid, 44
grapefruit, health benefits, 93, 135
guavas, health benefits, 135

honey
    Almond and Oatmeal Hotcakes with Honeyed Bananas, 30, 31
    health benefits, 31
    Italian Honey Nut Panforte, 46, 47

kumara
    Curried Kumara, Banana and Broccoli Salad, 78, 79
    health benefits, 39
    Kumara and Watercress Vichyssoise, 74, 75
    Kumara, Pumpkin and Split Pea Soup with Sesame Sage Pesto, 116, 117
    Orange-glazed Yams or Kumara, 86, 87
    Savoury Tarte Tatin, 118, 119

lamb, warm salad of soba noodles, steamed vegetables and, 122, 123
lentils
    Carrot and Lentil Soup, 94, 95
    Delicious Look-defying Lentil Salad, 38, 39
    health benefits, 128
    Moroccan Chicken Casserole, 140, 141
linseeds
    health benefits, 115
    My Magnificent Quick Muesli, 92, 93

Seedy Sprinkle, 138, 139
Simple Sweet Rollups, 114, 115

mangoes
    Favourite Fish with Lime Mint and Mango Salsa, 64, 65
    health benefits, 63, 64, 71
    Indian Chicken and Mango Stir-fry, 62, 63
    Skinful for Breakfast, 50, 51
Mediterranean Tart, 80, 81
Miso Vinaigrette, 97
Mocha Dessert Cake with Fresh Blueberry Sauce, 26, 27
muffins, banana and cracked wheat, 44, 45
muffins, toasted, with fresh fruit, 70, 71
mushrooms
    health benefits, 80, 143
    Mushroom and Spinach Risotto, 60, 61
    Roasted Mushrooms with Nutty Topping, 52, 53
    Steamed Fish Parcels with Bok Choy and Oyster Sauce, 142, 143
mussels, steamed, with Thai spices, 58, 59

New York Cheesecake, 130, 131
noodles
    Asian Seafood and Rice Noodle Soup, 34, 35
    Salmon and Noodle Salad, 56, 57
    Warm Soba Noodle Lamb and Steamed Vegetable Salad with Sesame Ginger Dressing, 122, 123
nuts – see also almonds; brazil nuts; walnuts
    Beetroot, Spinach and Broccoli Salad, 10, 11
    Crusty Salmon with Grilled Tomatoes and Oregano, 18, 19
    health benefits, 18, 36, 47, 52
    Pear and Apple Nut Crumble, 108, 109
    Simple Sweet Rollups, 114, 115
    Spiced Nuts, 148, 149

oats
    Almond and Oatmeal Hotcakes with Honeyed Bananas, 30, 31
    health benefits, 31, 109, 115
    My Magnificent Quick Muesli, 92, 93
    Pear and Apple Nut Crumble, 108, 109
    Skinful for Breakfast, 50, 51
onions
    health benefits, 64, 83, 101
    Middle Eastern Broccoli Crustless Quiche with Carrot and Poppy Seed Salad, 120, 121
    Warm Winter Salad with Orange and Walnut Vinaigrette, 100, 101
oranges
    Carrot, Orange and Banana Semolina Cake, 106, 107
    Date, Prune and Rhubarb Loaf, 88, 89
    health benefits, 36, 51, 71, 106
    Orange and Walnut Vinaigrette, 101
    Orange-glazed Yams or Kumara, 86, 87
    Skinful for Breakfast, 50, 51
pawpaw
    Fresh Pineapple Salsa for Chicken or Fish, 42, 43
    health benefits, 36, 63, 135
    Skinful for Breakfast, 50, 51
    Tarzan's Joint Juice, 32, 33
Pear and Apple Nut Crumble, 108, 109
pineapple, salsa for chicken or fish, 42, 43
prune, date, and rhubarb Loaf, 88, 89
pumpkin, kumara and split pea soup with sesame sage pesto, 116, 117

pumpkin seeds
    health benefits, 139, 140
    Moroccan Chicken Casserole, 140, 141
    Seedy Sprinkle, 138, 139

raisins
    health benefits, 110
    Sweet Raisin Treats, 110, 111
Raspberry Coulis, 130, 131
rhubarb, date and prune loaf, 88, 89

sage
    health benefits, 116
    Sesame Sage Pesto, 116
salads
    Avocado Skin-tonic Salad with Roasted Capsicum
        Vinaigrette, 54, 55
    Beetroot, Spinach and Broccoli Salad, 10, 11
    Carrot and Poppy Seed Salad, 120, 121
    Curried Kumara, Banana and Broccoli Salad, 78, 79
    Delicious Look-defying Lentil Salad, 38, 39
    Green Salad with Miso Vinaigrette, 96, 97
    Jack's Slaw, 136, 137
    Salmon and Noodle Salad, 56, 57
    Smoked Salmon, Avocado and Cucumber Salad, 98, 99
    Warm Soba Noodle Lamb and Steamed Vegetable Salad
        with Sesame Ginger Dressing, 122, 123
    Warm Winter Salad with Orange and Walnut Vinaigrette,
        100, 101
    Winter Fruit Salad, 72, 73
salmon
    Avocado and Smoked Salmon Pâté, 148, 149
    Crusty Salmon with Grilled Tomatoes and Oregano, 18, 19
    Salmon and Noodle Salad, 56, 57
    Salmon Puffs with Chopped Egg and Avocado, 40, 41
    Smoked Salmon, Avocado and Cucumber Salad, 98, 99
    Smoked Salmon, Spinach and Egg Pies, 16, 17
Sardine Lunch Toasties, 76, 77
seafood – see also fish
    Asian Seafood and Rice Noodle Soup, 34, 35
    Steamed Mussels with Thai Spices, 58, 59
Seedy Sprinkle, 138, 139
semolina cake, carrot, orange and banana, 106, 107
sesame seeds
    health benefits, 47, 139
    Italian Honey Nut Panforte, 46, 47
    Seedy Sprinkle, 138, 139
    Sesame Ginger Dressing, 123
    Sesame Sage Pesto, 116
soup
    Asian Seafood and Rice Noodle Soup, 34, 35
    Chicken and Vegetable Soup, 12, 13
    Green Goddess and Garlic Soup, 36, 37
    Kumara and Watercress Vichyssoise, 74, 75
    Kumara, Pumpkin and Split Pea Soup with Sesame Sage
        Pesto, 116, 117
    Roasted Tomato, Carrot and Capsicum Soup, 134, 135
sour cherries, health benefits, 32
soy products, health benefits, 51, 71, 128, 148
spinach
    Beetroot, Spinach and Broccoli Salad, 10, 11
    Fresh Tuna Loin with Wasabi and Anchovy Mayo, 20, 21
    Green Goddess and Garlic Soup, 36, 37
    health benefits, 17, 36, 52
    Mushroom and Spinach Risotto, 60, 61
    Roasted Mushrooms with Nutty Topping, 52, 53

Salmon and Noodle Salad, 56, 57
Sardine Lunch Toasties, 76, 77
Smoked Salmon, Spinach and Egg Pies, 16, 17
strawberries
    health benefits, 31
    Skinful for Breakfast, 50, 51
    Straw-Blue Fruit Smoothie, 8, 9
sweet potatoes – see kumara

tea
    green, 72
    health benefits, 67
    herbal and fruit, 115
    Winter Fruit Salad, 72, 73
tofu
    Avocado and Smoked Salmon Pâté, 148, 149
    health benefits, 119
    New York Cheesecake, 130, 131
    Savoury Tarte Tatin, 118, 119
tomatoes
    Crusty Salmon with Grilled Tomatoes and Oregano, 18, 19
    Fish Cakes with Indian Tomato Sauce, 14, 15
    health benefits, 83, 135, 140
    Mexican Beef Tortillas with Avocado Salsa, 82, 83
    Moroccan Chicken Casserole, 140, 141
    Roasted Tomato, Carrot and Capsicum Soup, 134, 135
tuna
    Asian Seafood and Rice Noodle Soup, 34, 35
    Fish Cakes with Indian Tomato Sauce, 14, 15
    Fresh Tuna Loin with Wasabi and Anchovy Mayo, 20, 21
    health benefits, 35
turmeric
    Fish Cakes with Indian Tomato Sauce, 14, 15
    health benefits, 14, 39

vegetables – see also specific vegetables, e.g. broccoli
    Chicken and Vegetable Soup, 12, 13
    Green Salad with Miso Vinaigrette, 96, 97
    health benefits, 25, 60, 97
    Steamed Greens with Seedy Sprinkle, 138, 139
    Stir-fried Vietnamese Beef, 126, 127
    Vegetable Curry, 144, 145
    Warm Soba Noodle Lamb and Steamed Vegetable Salad
        with Sesame Ginger Dressing, 122, 123
    Warm Winter Salad with Orange and Walnut Vinaigrette,
        100, 101

walnuts
    Date, Prune and Rhubarb Loaf, 88, 89
    health benefits, 88
    Orange and Walnut Vinaigrette, 101
    Roasted Mushrooms with Nutty Topping, 52, 53
Wasabi and Anchovy Mayo, 20, 21
watercress
    Green Goddess and Garlic Soup, 36, 37
    health benefits, 60
    Kumara and Watercress Vichyssoise, 74, 75
    Salmon and Noodle Salad, 56, 57
watermelon, health benefits, 135

yams
    health benefits, 123
    Orange-glazed Yams or Kumara, 86, 87